For Jack Garland
W. M.

For my parents
P.B.

First published 1984 by
Walker Books Ltd
184-192 Drummond Street
London NW1 3HP

Text © 1984 William Mayne
Illustrations © 1984 Patrick Benson

First printed 1984
Printed and bound by L.E.G.O., Vicenza, Italy

British Library Cataloguing in Publication Data
Mayne, William
The yellow book of Hob stories.
I. Title II. Benson, Patrick
823'.914[J] PZ7

ISBN 0-7445-0122-9

THE YELLOW BOOK OF

HOB
STORIES

WILLIAM MAYNE

ILLUSTRATED BY PATRICK BENSON

WALKER BOOKS
LONDON

HOB AND EGGY PALMER

Boy and Girl know that Hob is there. The family feels complete when he comes out to sit with them.

Tonight he shyly squats on the hardest cushion, furthest from the fire. All the cushions are hard tonight.

'He's here,' says Girl. She does not look in case she frightens him.

'He's there,' says Boy. He does not point. It would not be polite.

'Nonsense,' says Mr. 'And it's time to go to bed.'

Boy and Girl go to bed. 'Good night, Hob,' they say.

Hob has just got up, from his cutch, or cupboard, underneath the stairs. Hob thinks there is a problem in the house.

'Did you lay an egg, Budgie?' he asks, when they are alone.

Budgie blushes. 'Not me,' she whispers.

'Good,' says Hob. He knows there is an eggy problem.

'What a thing to ask!' says Budgie.

When the family is all in bed Hob finds what is wrong.

Someone has been boiling eggs. Baby had an egg for tea.

In the water the egg had cracked. Eggy Palmer had come out. First a long white finger. Then a broad white hand.

Then Eggy Palmer his full self came swimming from the shell, hard and ready, ready and set.

'Set and go, Hob thinks,' says Hob.

Eggy Palmer waits in the kitchen to make the custard lumpy. He will dip his broad smooth hand in it and spoil it.

He will put bones in the potatoes.

He will put long blobs like cloth in the milk.

He will stain spoons black and put hard lumps between forks.

He will make spaghetti stick together.

He will make jelly lumpy.

He has already been in the cushions.

Now he is in the sink, using his brain, having a think beside the drain.

Hob thinks too. Eggy Palmer will have to go. But Hob does not tell him so, because that might make him cross.

Hob is kind to him. Beware of Hob when Hob is being nice. It is best when Hob speaks sharply to you, very near unkind.

'I'll help you out of there,' says Hob. 'You might get washed away.'

'Thank you,' says Eggy Palmer. 'Then I can get to work.'

'Just climb in this eggshell, where you came from,' says Hob. 'I'll lift you from the sink.'

Eggy Palmer climbs in. Hob puts his thumb on top to keep him in. 'Hob knows,' says Hob, and goes to the waterside and sends Eggy down the stream, away and away.

'How far to custard?' shouts Eggy.

Of course it is very far. But Eggy comes out happy, and he is quite good for frogspawn.

Hob goes home. He eats his gift, a roasted apple. There is something knotted in the middle. It is the core. Budgie eats the pips.

HOB AND SOOTKIN

Who sat by the fire one icy winter's morning, puffing an old clay pipe?

'Who is it?' says Mr. 'I smell a sort of goblin tobacco.'

'It's Hob,' says Girl. 'I know the smell.'

'It's Hob,' says Boy. 'It's cold today.'

'It's Hob,' says Hob. 'Hob has been found out, so he'll go back to his cutch underneath the stairs.'

Hob goes to his cupboard so quick, before he's seen, that he leaves the old clay pipe behind.

'You've frightened him away,' says Girl.

'There was nothing there,' says Mr.

But Boy puts the old clay pipe in a safe place. He knows and Girl knows. Hob knows.

That night there is worse than goblin tobacco making smoke.

The chimney is not working well. Puffs of smoke go up, but puffs of smoke come down. Puffs of smoke are in the room.

'All those smuts,' says Mrs. 'And Baby turning black.'

Smoke gets in their eyes.

Budgie coughs. 'I'm trying to give it up,' she says.

The family goes to bed. Budgie puts her head under her wing. The air is fresher there.

Hob comes out. He thinks it is his fault. He goes to find his old clay pipe.

He finds it. He expects the smoke has come from that. But it is not so.

He goes to the fireplace. Smoke comes down. Hob gets it in his mouth. It gets in his ears.

It seems to speak to him.

'Hob hears you,' says Hob. 'Your name is Sootkin. You live in the chimney.'

Sootkin rustles in the chimney. Black specks fall down.

'You will have to go,' says Hob.

Sootkin shakes a chimney pot. 'Never,' says Sootkin.

'Hob says yes,' says Hob.

Sootkin scampers up and down the flue. Lumps of black fall down and smell foul.

'Hob thinks what to do,' says Hob.

He remembers then. He knows. The cure is something he does not like, but he bravely touches it. He brings salt from the salt pot, and sprinkles it on Sootkin's toes.

Sootkin does not like it either. He whizzes round and round.

Hob sprinkles salt on Sootkin's head.

Sootkin roars. Sootkin rushes out of the top of the chimney. He goes so fast the chimney pot splits apart and falls.

'Hob is pleased,' says Hob.

Budgie brings her head out and spits black spit.

Hob sweeps up. When that is done he finds his gift, a mug of ale. 'That slakes the soot,' he says.

In the morning Mr finds the broken chimney pot and thinks that that was what was wrong. Hob knows better.

HOB AND HINKY PUNK

Hob likes the twilight at dusk and dawn. He sees best then, and can be seen. Bright day and black dark are not good for him.

'We see him in the shadows,' says Boy.

'Or moonlight,' says his sister, Girl.

'Just when I've got my eyes closed,' shouts Budgie.

'You're all talking nonsense,' says Mr.

Hob listens from his cupboard. 'They are talking about Hob,' says Hob.

At night he creeps from his cutch, his cupboard.

He waits. Budgie snores. A mouse comes out and asks for quiet.

In a corner of the room something seems to grow out of the stone floor. Little things like leaves of grass come up, blue and bright, red and shining, long and longer.

It is not grass, but hair. And the head comes out, and the rest of a little creature, all bright and shining.

Hob shades his eyes. 'And who are you?' he asks.

'I'm Hinky Punk,' the creature says.

Budgie wakes. 'Go away,' she says.

'Go to roost, sparrow,' says Hinky Punk. He says to Hob, 'What's up, Grandad? You don't have to stay. Hinky Punk rules OK.'

'This is Hob's home,' says Hob.

And the mice say, 'This is our mousehold. Bless this mouse.'

'Hinky Punk has come to town,' says Hinky Punk. 'I was getting nowhere in the swamp. Here I am until I leave.'

'What shall we do?' ask the mice.

Budgie bites her nails.

Hob shuts his eyes and thinks.

Hinky Punk goes running round the room, jumping on the table, clattering in the hearth, being so bright.

'Vandal,' says Budgie.

Hob thinks.

'Candle,' says Budgie.

Baby wakes and cries.

'Scandal,' says Budgie.

'Featherbrain,' says Hob. He is thinking. Then he has thought.

He talks to the mice. He explains what they can do. 'It's the same for Hinky Punk as it is for Hob,' he says. 'Just as it was for Black Dog.'

The mice begin their work. 'It is a secret,' they tell Hinky Punk, when he comes round to watch. 'Stand there so we can see to thread the needle.'

They thread and they sew, and they cut and they stitch, and their mousework is a suit of clothes for Hinky Punk. He has to put them on.

'Good gear,' he says.

And when he has them on he has to go. 'Cheers,' he says, and stamps off in new boots.

'Good riddance,' say the mice, and Budgie, and Hob.

HOB AND SLEEPYHEAD

Hob looks with a bright eye through the spyhole in his cutch or cupboard.

'Something is looking out,' says Mrs. 'It will be a spider. Ugh.'

'Hob looked out,' says Boy.

'He lives there in his cutch,' says Girl.

'Hob looked out,' says Hob. 'But he doesn't see so well.'

'I can't see anything,' says Mr.

'You're worse than me,' says Hob. 'And I have a headache too.'

Girl says, 'I am so sleepy.'

Baby nods his head.

Mr closes his eyes.

Boy gazes into the fire.

Budgie says she is losing her mind.

'I know,' says Hob.

Mrs knits three stitches backwards in the wrong colour on the poker instead of the needle. 'How tired I am,' she says. 'We'll all go to bed.'

Hob gets up. His poor head aches. Budgie sits with eyes tight closed, too weary to put her head under her wing.

Hob thinks he is dreaming.

Then he thinks that something is dreaming him.

Hob thinks his headache is too bad. He goes upstairs and wakes Mrs. She gives him headache tea, and he feels better then.

He looks in the mirror. He sees his face. It looks and feels fuzzy. He sees on his head a round black thing like a little hat. He knows it is not clothes. But what is it?

He takes it off and sees it is Sleepyhead. Sleepyhead has put a hand on everyone and made them sleep – Mr, Mrs, Baby, Boy, Girl, Budgie and the mouse.

Hob stayed awake and his head hurt.

'What are you doing here?' he asks. 'Hob wants to know. His eyes want mending or he would have seen you sooner.'

'I have to sleep somewhere,' says Sleepyhead. 'But hedgehogs prickled me and woke me up. I'll sleep here, Hob.'

'This is Hob's house,' says Hob.

'Don't send me back to hedgehogs,' says Sleepyhead. 'They have spiny dreams.'

'Hob will help,' says Hob, and goes looking for help.

There is Dormouse in the shed. 'I can't sleep,' he says. 'Will Mrs give me sleeping tea?'

'Hob gives you this,' says Hob, and puts Sleepyhead beside him. They curl up together, snore and snore alike.

Hob's headache goes. Inside, beside the fire, he finds his present, a pair of glasses. Now he can see sharp again. He looks at Budgie.

'It's a monster,' Budgie shouts, and rings her bell.

In the morning Mrs asks which child had headache tea at night.

'It was Hob,' say Boy and Girl. 'He says thank you very much.'

'I do,' says Hob, sleepy in his cutch.

HOB AND TOOTH FAIRY

Who had bad dreams in a cupboard under the stairs?

'It's Hob,' say Boy and Girl. 'That's his cutch, where he lives.'

'It's the drains,' says Mr. 'Drains are real, at least.'

Hob was dreaming. He dreams all day, in his sleep. Sometimes he wakes up.

'Nothing like a good dream,' he says.

Baby dreams at night. Baby wakes.

'That was bad dream,' says Baby. Baby tells the house.

'Poor thing,' says Mrs. 'His teeth are coming through. Look.'

Hob says, 'Perhaps Hob's teeth are coming through. Here's a gap, and there's a gap.' But perhaps Hob's teeth are like that.

Girl puts a finger tip in her mouth and smiles round it. 'I have a loose tooth,' she says. 'Feel it wobbling.'

'We have a problem,' says Hob. Girl lets him feel her tooth. She trusts him. He trusts her. The tooth is loose backwards and forwards.

'Hob has work to do,' says Hob.

Next he looks in Baby's mouth. There is a little lump, but the tooth has not come up. Hob rubs the place and Baby dribbles with delight.

He looks inside Girl's smile. The tooth is loose up and down. Hob knows what to do and looks for the thing to do it with. Girl's tooth hangs by a thread.

Baby is extremely cross.

'A toothling, not a changeling,' says Hob. He has to go on looking for what he needs.

Baby gets a rash. Girl says she cannot eat anything she does not like, with a tooth like that.

Hob finds a silver thing he wants. Now he is ready. He waits.

Suddenly Girl says, 'It has gone. It has fallen out.' There on the table lies her tooth.

'Ah,' says Hob, still waiting.

'Eat your potato, Girl,' says Mrs.

Baby's rash vanishes. In his mouth is a little white bud, a tooth coming up.

Everybody looks. Boy and Girl think the little bud may open like a flower.

Hob is busy. He knows what came out with Girl's tooth, and flew up to settle near Budgie, waiting for a new home. Hob sees Tooth Fairy.

'Is it here?' asks Tooth Fairy, looking longingly at Budgie.

'No,' says Hob. 'It lost its teeth long ago.' Budgie hears that and snarls. Hob takes the Fairy down to Baby, and Baby smiles.

'Pay for my old tooth,' says Fairy, 'and I'll go to work again, growing a new set for Baby.'

Hob takes the silver thing, a coin, and puts it where Girl has left her tooth, in a glass of water.

His gift tonight is a long white pipe, a yard of clay. It fits the gap in his teeth, better than a tooth.

Upstairs Mr's teeth are in a glass of water. He will never get a silver penny for any of them.